STAR WARS®

ATTACK OF THE CLONES™
SCRAPBOOK

WRITTEN BY RYDER WINDHAM

INTERIOR DESIGN BY JASON ZAMAJTUK

RANDOM HOUSE NEW YORK

LUCAS BOOKS

CONTENTS

Special thanks to the following people
for their work on this book.
At Lucas Licensing Ltd.:
Lucy Autrey Wilson
Jonathan W. Rinzler
Chris Cerasi
Iain Morris

At Random House Children's Books:
Alice Alfonsi
Jason Zamajtuk
Kerry Milliron
Lisa Findlay
Artie Bennett
Jenny Golub
Christopher Shea
Stephanie Finnegan
Colleen Fellingham
Milton Wackerow
Amy Bowman
Carol Naughton

Published in the United States by Random House, Inc., New York,
and simultaneously in Canada by Random House of Canada Limited, Toronto.
www.randomhouse.com/kids

Official Star Wars Web Sites: www.starwars.com   www.starwarskids.com

Library of Congress Control Number: 2001098800   ISBN: 0-375-81582-1
Printed in the United States of America   First Edition April 2002   10 9 8 7 6 5 4 3 2 1

INTRODUCTION

In the first *Star Wars* film, released in 1977, the world met one of the most memorable characters ever to appear in a motion picture: the villainous Sith Lord Darth Vader. We didn't know much about the mysterious Vader, only that before he turned to the dark side, he had been a Jedi Knight.

That first *Star Wars* adventure, which was later retitled *Star Wars*: Episode IV—*A New Hope*, was followed by Episode V: *The Empire Strikes Back* (1980) and Episode VI: *Return of the Jedi* (1983). These films made motion-picture history, breaking box-office records and setting new standards for visual effects. Now, creator George Lucas is going back before the events of the classic *Star Wars* trilogy to tell us Anakin's story.

Episode I: *The Phantom Menace* (1999) introduced Anakin as a good-hearted nine-year-old boy. If you had a hard time imagining that the young and innocent Anakin would grow up to be Darth Vader, that was what filmmaker George Lucas intended: "The whole point is—and the reason I started the story where I did—is that Anakin is a normal kid, a good kid. And how does somebody who is normal and good turn bad? What are the qualities, what is it that we all have within us, that can turn us bad?"

If you've seen the end of this saga (Episode VI: *Return of the Jedi*), you already know what happens to Anakin—and that good ultimately triumphs over evil. However, there are many twists and turns along the path that leads Anakin to his destiny, and as of Episode II, the journey isn't over yet. So once again, let us go back a long time ago, to a galaxy far, far away. . . .

THE JEDI

Soon after returning from one of their missions, a border dispute on Ansion, Obi-Wan Kenobi and Anakin Skywalker are assigned to protect Senator Padmé Amidala from mysterious assassins.

MASTER AND APPRENTICE

The Jedi are an Order of wise and powerful knights. For 25,000 years they have served as the guardians of peace and justice in the Republic, the galaxy's democratic union of star systems. The Jedi draw their strength and vision from the Force, an energy field generated by all living things. The Jedi manipulate this energy to achieve their noble goals.

A Jedi is typically identified within six months of his or her birth, and is raised at the Jedi Temple on the planet Coruscant. An important step in a Jedi's training is becoming a Padawan, or apprentice, under the tutelage of a Jedi Knight or Master. A Padawan who passes the trials becomes a Jedi Knight, and a Jedi Knight who accomplishes specific tasks—such as successfully training a Padawan—becomes a Jedi Master.

You haven't learned anything.
—Obi-Wan to Anakin

Courageous and disciplined, Obi-Wan Kenobi first trained at the Jedi Temple under Jedi Master Yoda and then apprenticed with Jedi Master Qui-Gon Jinn. Obi-Wan's ascension from Padawan to Jedi Knight took place the moment he summoned the Force to defeat the evil Darth Maul in a lightsaber duel.

The Sith Lord Maul had already mortally wounded Qui-Gon by the time Obi-Wan's final blow was struck, and in his last dying moments, Qui-Gon asked Obi-Wan to train Anakin Skywalker to become a Jedi Knight. Obi-Wan promised to fulfill his Master's final wish and made Anakin his apprentice.

For the past ten years, Obi-Wan has diligently taught and guided Anakin, developing a deep affection for the boy as together they have completed a number of missions throughout the galaxy. Although Anakin has shown great promise, Obi-Wan still has many concerns about the teen's headstrong nature and rebellious streak. Constant reminders of basic lessons are wearing thin for both of them, yet Obi-Wan remains determined to fulfill his promise to Qui-Gon and complete Anakin's training.

PLAYING OBI-WAN

Ewan McGregor reprises his Episode I role as Obi-Wan Kenobi. "To be a part of a legend, to be a part of a modern myth, and to play the young Alec Guinness is an incredible honor." Alec Guinness played the elderly Obi-Wan "Ben" Kenobi in *Star Wars*: Episode IV—*A New Hope*.

"Someday I will be the most powerful Jedi ever."
—Anakin Skywalker

ANAKIN SKYWALKER

At the age of nine, Anakin Skywalker was living as a slave on the remote desert planet Tatooine when he was discovered by Jedi Master Qui-Gon Jinn. Qui-Gon saw that Anakin possessed great powers and came to believe that the boy was the "chosen one" of Jedi prophecy, destined to bring balance to the Force.

The Jedi Council tested Anakin and ruled he was too old to begin the training, too full of fear. But after Qui-Gon Jinn's death, the Council reversed their decision and allowed the boy to become a Padawan to Obi-Wan Kenobi.

Now, at the age of nineteen, Anakin is a prodigy. His Force abilities are impressive, and he is the best star pilot at the Jedi Temple. Yet Anakin is not entirely happy as a Padawan. He is haunted by dark visions about his mother, who remained behind as a slave on Tatooine. And although he loves Master Obi-Wan like a father, Anakin must fight his impatience with the slow pace of his training. He sometimes thinks that Obi-Wan is holding him back from reaching his greatest potential.

PLAYING ANAKIN

Hayden Christensen makes his *Star Wars* debut as Anakin Skywalker. A fan since childhood, he admits, "I always was curious what Darth Vader was going to look like under the mask."

Anakin's Lightsaber

Anakin was at the top of his class in lightsaber training at the Jedi Temple. At age thirteen, he constructed this lightsaber in the Crystal Cave on the planet Ilum, using three blue crystals to focus the energy from the weapon's power cell. The crystals' color is extended through the lightsaber's blade.

Obi-Wan's Lightsaber

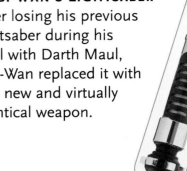

After losing his previous lightsaber during his duel with Darth Maul, Obi-Wan replaced it with this new and virtually identical weapon.

Tracer Beacon (Tracking device)

When attached to his adversary's transport, this device emits a signal to Obi-Wan, allowing him to track the craft across space.

Obi-Wan's Electrobinoculars

Whether the atmosphere is blindingly bright, dense with fog, or pitch-black, Obi-Wan's multi-sensor binoculars allow him to bring distant objects into sharp focus.

Jedi Starfighter

Officially known as a Delta-7 *Aethersprite* light interceptor, the Jedi starfighter is a wedge-shaped, single-person craft equipped with dual laser cannons and a powerful deflector shield. Although a craft of this small size cannot hold a standard hyperdrive, the Jedi starfighter is able to travel into deep space by virtue of a booster and an Astromech Droid for navigation.

R4-P17

"Arfour" is the Astromech Droid who serves as Obi-Wan's co-pilot on the Jedi starfighter. Instead of a truncated conical head like other R4 units, this R4 (thanks to some retrofitting by Anakin Skywalker) has a domed head like an R2 unit, and it is hardwired into the ship.

PLAYING VADER

Anakin Skywalker and Obi-Wan Kenobi have been played by several different actors over the course of the *Star Wars* saga.

Episode I: *The Phantom Menace*—Anakin (Jake Lloyd) first meets Obi-Wan (Ewan McGregor) on the Naboo Royal Starship.

Episode II: *Attack of the Clones*—Anakin (Hayden Christensen) and Obi-Wan (Ewan McGregor) consult with Padmé on Coruscant.

"We meet again, at last."
—Darth Vader to Obi-Wan,
Episode IV: *A New Hope*

Episode IV: *A New Hope*—An aged Obi-Wan (Alec Guinness) combats Darth Vader (with the body of David Prowse, voice of James Earl Jones, and heavy breathing by sound designer Ben Burtt).

Episode VI: *Return of the Jedi*—Anakin (Sebastian Shaw) and Obi-Wan (Alec Guinness) are reunited as spiritual entities.

JEDI TEMPLE

Elevated above a low-rise sector of Galactic City on Coruscant, the Jedi Temple is where Jedi train and reside. The stepped architectural style of its base is intended to symbolize the Padawan's path to enlightenment in the Force. The Temple is topped by five towers, one of which houses the Jedi High Council.

DRAWING BOARD
Inspired by the TransAmerica pyramid and the San Francisco skyline, Episode I concept designer Doug Chiang and concept artist Edwin Natividad incorporated Gothic, Art Deco, and ancient Chinese and Egyptian architectural styles into the design of the Jedi Temple.

THE BEAR CLAN
Young Jedi aged four to eight belong to one of ten different clans. Master Yoda instructs each of those clans. In *Attack of the Clones,* we see him instructing the Bear Clan, which consists of twenty Jedi children.

JEDI TEMPLE ARCHIVES LIBRARY

Lighted computer panels appear to stretch to infinity within the Jedi Temple Archives Library, which contains extensive archives for the hundreds of thousands of known systems in the galaxy. The library also includes the most complete collection of works related to Jedi history.

DRAWING BOARD

Lucasfilm concept artists designed the Jedi Temple Archives Library (with its vaulted ceilings, stately architecture, and busts of famous living and dead Jedi) after studying a number of legendary libraries, from the Vatican's to those found on old English estates.

"If an item does not appear in our records, it does not exist."—Madame Jocasta Nu

MADAME JOCASTA NU

An elderly human female Jedi, Madame Jocasta Nu is in charge of maintaining the Jedi Temple Archives Library. Over the years, countless Jedi have come to her for assistance in looking up everything from navigational charts to information on alien languages and customs.

THE LOST TWENTY

In the long history of the Jedi, only twenty have ever left the Order. Known as the "Lost Twenty," their last addition was Count Dooku. After leaving the Order and disappearing ten years ago, he recently emerged as a political activist leading the Separatist movement.

JEDI MAP ROOM

The Jedi map room has information about every planet and star. And the Jedi analysis room is used to examine artifacts, which often hold clues to questions that may come up during assigned missions.

The Jedi Council

All matters related to the Jedi are controlled by the Jedi High Council, which has twelve members. Each of the High Council's members is a respected and experienced Jedi Knight who has probably achieved the designation of Jedi Master.

Adi Gallia
Just prior to the crisis on Geonosis, Adi Gallia was flying a new prototype of the Jedi starfighter to aid the resistance movement in the Karthakk system. Her former Padawan, Siri Tachi, has also established herself as a formidable Jedi.

Oppo Rancisis
A Thisspian, Oppo Rancisis is a cunning military strategist with a superior tactical mind.

Even Piell
With the heritage of a Lannik warrior, Even Piell is fearless in battle.

Shaak Ti
Jedi Master Shaak Ti is a Togruta from Shili. Many species are under the impression that Togrutas are venomous, but this is only a myth. However, it is not a myth that Master Shaak Ti discourages.

Saesee Tiin
An Iktotchi with natural telepathic abilities, Jedi Master Saesee Tiin is a daring star pilot. In fact, he is a test pilot for a newer-model Jedi starfighter—an improved version of the ship Obi-Wan uses to travel from Coruscant to Kamino.

Coleman Trebor
An amphibious Vurk, Coleman Trebor is from the watery world of Sembla. He has peacefully resolved several major planetary disputes, but if called upon to draw his lightsaber, this Jedi Master does so without fail.

Eeth Koth
Jedi Master Eeth Koth is a Zabrak. After he heard reports that Qui-Gon Jinn's slayer might have been an Iridonian Zabrak, Eeth Koth conducted an extensive investigation, but he has yet to discover the identity of the deceased Sith Lord.

KI-ADI-MUNDI
A Cerean with a binary brain, Ki-Adi-Mundi was a Jedi Knight at the time of the Battle of Naboo, and the only member of the Council who was not a Jedi Master. Since then, he has trained a Padawan through knighthood and has become a Jedi Master.

YODA
The Council's eldest and wisest member.

MACE WINDU
A senior member of the High Council.

DEPA BILLABA
While her allies race to Geonosis, Depa Billaba is assigned to remain on Coruscant and supervise the young Jedi clans.

PLO KOON
Jedi Master Plo Koon is a Kel Dor from Dorin and, thus, wears goggles and an antiox mask to protect him from oxygen-rich atmospheres. A courageous warrior, he is also respected for his vast scientific knowledge.

Mace Windu & Yoda

MACE WINDU

A senior member of the High Council, Jedi Master Mace Windu is concerned by the growing disturbance in the Force and the fate of the Republic. He knows there may not be a peaceful way to resolve the problems presented by the Separatist movement. When Mace Windu learns that the Separatists have assembled a droid army on Geonosis, he decides to lead a battalion of Jedi to the distant world.

"There aren't enough Jedi to protect the Republic. We are keepers of the peace, not soldiers."—Mace Windu

PLAYING MACE

Samuel L. Jackson returns to the role of Mace Windu. In Episode II, he notes that his character "seems to be the second most powerful Jedi on the Council, next to Yoda. . . . I usually describe Mace as a voice of reason. He thinks before he speaks. He's pretty calculating, mostly even-tempered. And he's not to be trifled with."

JEDI IN ACTION

Financed by the Republic government, the Jedi are sent on missions throughout the galaxy. Because the Jedi are spread out light-years apart on worlds that require their presence, it can be difficult or even disastrous for them to abandon their assignments. When the Republic learns the Separatists have gathered a massive army to wage a civil war, only about one hundred Jedi are available to intervene. Shown here are just a few of the Jedi who help.

KIT FISTO
A Nautolan from Glee Anselm, Jedi Master Kit Fisto is an amphibious Jedi. With his enhanced sense of smell, he is easily able to detect pheromones and the slightest changes in the body chemistry of others.

BULTAR SWAN
Skilled in the acrobatic style of Jedi combat, Jedi Knight Bultar Swan has never taken a life, but she acknowledges that the day may come when an enemy will leave her no choice.

"The dark side clouds everything. Impossible to see, the future is. But this I am sure of. Do their duty, the Jedi will."
—Yoda

YODA

At over eight hundred years old, Jedi Master Yoda is the Council's eldest and wisest member. Usually able to use the Force to anticipate future events, Yoda now finds his insights clouded by the emergence of the dark side. Despite his age and relatively small size, he is one of the most powerful Jedi Masters and has every intention of joining his allies in the fight against the Separatists' army.

STASS ALLIE

Jedi Knight Stass Allie is an experienced warrior but is increasingly devoted to the Circle of Jedi Healers. As a battle on Geonosis presents the possibility of casualties, she is determined to do everything in her power to aid her allies. Stass Allie's cousin is Jedi Master Adi Gallia.

LUMINARA UNDULI

Luminara Unduli is from Mirial, a cold desert world. The Mirialans wear tattoos to denote cultural concepts of their destinies. She recently participated in negotiations on Ansion with Obi-Wan Kenobi, Anakin Skywalker, and her Padawan, Barriss Offee.

BARRISS OFFEE

Barriss Offee is apprenticed to Luminara Unduli. Like her Master, Barriss is also from Mirial. As there has been at least one Mirialan Jedi at all times for the last several hundred years, Barriss knows she represents a long and strong tradition.

The Sith Order was founded thousands of years ago by renegade Jedi who had embraced the dark side of the Force. Instead of using the Force to serve those in need, the Sith used their powers for domination. Consumed by their own evil, many of the original Sith destroyed each other, and most who survived were hunted down by the Jedi. In the end, only one Sith Master remained.

To prevent any future conflicts between apprentices, the surviving Master decreed that no Sith Master should ever again take on more than one apprentice at a time. From then on, their evil ways have been passed down in absolute secrecy. Their restricted number concealed their existence as they waited for the perfect time to emerge again and strike back at the Jedi and the Republic in which they flourish.

Until the Jedi Master Qui-Gon Jinn was confronted by a Sith Lord on Tatooine, the Jedi had long believed the Sith Order was extinct. In the ten years since the Battle of Naboo, the Jedi have remained watchful for any additional evidence of the Sith's existence.

DARTH SIDIOUS

From his secret lair on Coruscant, the mysterious Sith Lord Darth Sidious schemes to have complete control of the galaxy, manipulating events toward his evil goal. Although Darth Sidious lost his apprentice, Darth Maul, during the Battle of Naboo, he quickly found a new and most resourceful apprentice.

DARTH TYRANUS

In the ten years since Darth Maul's demise, Darth Tyranus has served as apprentice to Darth Sidious. Although Darth Tyranus's true identity is shrouded in mystery, known only by Darth Sidious and Jango Fett, it may not be a coincidence that he first emerged at about the same time Count Dooku left the Jedi Order.

NAMING THE SITH

In George Lucas's rough draft of the first *Star Wars* script, "Jedi Bendu" warriors battled the "Knights of Sith." In later drafts, the dark Order was referred to as the "Legion of Lettow," but the focus shifted to a single warrior: Darth Vader, Dark Lord of the Sith.

"The time will come when that cult of greed called the Republic will lose even the pretext of democracy and freedom."—Count Dooku

COUNT DOOKU'S LIGHTSABER

In the elegant, seemingly effortless "old style" of lightsaber fencing, Count Dooku has no match. Despite his advanced years, he continues to wield his curved, red-bladed weapon with lethal accuracy.

GEONOSIAN SPEEDER

During the battle on Geonosis, Count Dooku pilots this personal, open-cockpit vehicle.

COUNT DOOKU

Although he does not identify himself as a Sith, Count Dooku did abandon the Jedi Order. Once a Jedi Master who mentored Qui-Gon Jinn, Dooku is now a political activist. He is outspoken in his support of the Separatist movement, a group of several thousand solar systems that intend to leave the Republic and form a separate government. Dooku believes that the Jedi Order has lowered itself by willingly serving what has become a corrupt Republic, mired in the bickering of self-serving politicians. He even claims that Supreme Chancellor Palpatine may be under the control of a Sith Lord.

PLAYING DOOKU

This is not the first time actor Christopher Lee has played a count. His many memorable film roles have included Count Dracula, the Frankenstein monster, Sherlock Holmes, and—most recently—Saruman the White in *The Lord of the Rings: The Fellowship of the Ring*. He has also appeared in many films with actor Peter Cushing, who played Grand Moff Tarkin in Episode IV: *A New Hope*. Lee recalls, "I wrote him a letter saying, 'What on earth is a Grand Moff?' He wrote back and said, 'I have no idea!'"

COUNT DOOKU'S SOLAR SAILER

For interstellar journeys, such as the route between Geonosis and Coruscant, Dooku uses his Solar Sailer. The most remarkable feature of this *Punworcca* 116-class interstellar sloop is its solar sail. Attached by Geonosian engineers, the sail is Dooku's find: a reflector-surfaced apparatus used to power and drive the ship across space with almost no other source of fuel.

Concept art of Solar Sailer by Doug Chiang

THE SEPARATISTS

The Separatist movement, officially named the Confederacy of Independent Systems, is committed to capitalism and the eventual abolition of all trade barriers. As an outspoken leader in the movement, Count Dooku has built alliances with representatives of the interstellar commerce factions, and is attempting to convince them that if they sign the Separatist treaty, they will gain profits beyond their wildest dreams. With the support of these leaders, Dooku believes a thousand more systems will leave the Republic and join his cause.

NUTE GUNRAY

A Neimoidian, Nute is Viceroy for the Trade Federation. He insists that he will not sign a treaty with the Separatists until Senator Amidala's head is served up on his desk. She was instrumental in his embarrassing defeat on Naboo, and he's hungry for revenge.

POGGLE THE LESSER

Poggle is the Archduke of Geonosis. Under his leadership, the Geonosians have agreed to build an army of Battle Droids for each Separatist group, including the Trade Federation.

PASSEL ARGENTE

A Koorivar, Passel is both the Republic Senator of Kooriva and the Magistrate for the Corporate Alliance. Tainted by his wealth and private interests, Argente openly defies the Republic by joining the Separatists.

BEHIND THE MASKS

Silas Carson plays two characters in Episode II: the cowering Nute Gunray and the Jedi Master Ki-Adi-Mundi. "With Ki-Adi, I enjoy playing this very wise man who is part of the great Council. You get the feeling he is kind of like your uncle, because he's this nice, kind, wise, protective Master. Nute is a completely different character altogether, but he makes me laugh because he's such a coward. . . . There is something dreadfully vulnerable about him."

SAN HILL

A Muun from Muunilinst, San Hill is the Chairman of the InterGalactic Banking Clan. With its nonexclusive arrangement to support Count Dooku, the greedy Clan hopes to profit from the coming galactic war by funding arms sales to both the Separatists and the Republic.

SHU MAI

Shu Mai is President of the Commerce Guild. Although the Commerce Guild does not wish to be seen as being involved with the Separatists, it agrees to support Count Dooku in secret.

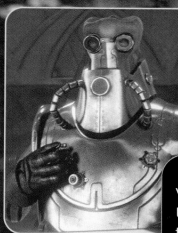

WAT TAMBOR

Wat Tambor is Foreman of the Techno Union, the premier developer of emerging technologies. Unable to breathe air, he requires a high-pressure gas mask to survive on Geonosis.

COUNT DOOKU

A former Jedi Master, the Count is now the leader in the dangerous Separatist movement.

![Super Battle Droid logo]

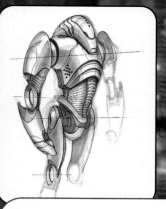

DRAWING BOARD

"The aesthetic of the new Super Battle Droid is that it's both machine and weapon," says Lucasfilm concept designer Doug Chiang, who created the above concept art. "The leading edges of the arms and legs are like knife blades."

SUPER BATTLE DROIDS

More threatening than and far superior to the Trade Federation's previous Battle Droids, as seen in Episode I, Super Battle Droids carry greater firepower and operate autonomously, without the remote aid of a Droid Control Ship. Like other droids, their electronic brains are not organic, so they cannot be affected by Jedi mind tricks.

THE SENATE

For many centuries, the galaxy's center of government has been located in Galactic City on the planet Coruscant. There, an immense domed building, two kilometers in diameter, houses the Galactic Senate, which includes representatives from thousands of member star systems.

An alarming number of Senate representatives have already chosen to join the Separatists. However, the Republic has managed to retain a great many loyal Senators, who have become known as Loyalists.

The Jedi have for years been able to maintain peace by themselves. Yet even their High Council members warn the Senate that there are not enough Jedi to fight a war for the Republic.

Many believe it is finally time for the Republic to approve the creation of an army. The only way for that to happen, however, is if the Senate approves the Military Creation Act, and the Loyalists are bitterly divided about whether such a vote would strengthen unity or shatter what remains of the Republic.

SUPREME CHANCELLOR PALPATINE

Formerly the Senator of Naboo, Palpatine became Supreme Chancellor of the Galactic Senate after Queen Amidala moved for a vote of no confidence concerning the previous Chancellor, Finis Valorum. In the decade since the Battle of Naboo, the Trade Federation has continued to seize control of defenseless worlds, and the Senate has become increasingly stagnant. Since the Separatist movement first emerged, Palpatine has attempted to hold off the motion to vote on forming an army for the Republic. However, for many, it is clear the time is coming when an army will be needed. As more systems join the Separatists, Palpatine gives every appearance that he is working to maintain order in the Senate.

"I will not let this Republic that has stood for a thousand years be split in two."
—Supreme Chancellor Palpatine

PLAYING PALPATINE

Ian McDiarmid first played Palpatine in Episode VI: *Return of the Jedi* and has developed unique insight into the character. "Palpatine appears to be a hardworking politician. . . . But at the same time, I know that underneath all that is an evil soul. The undercurrents are always there in his mind and in his gut."

THE LOYALISTS

A courageous Loyalist, Senator Bail Organa is the head of the royal family of Alderaan, a planet that—like Senator Amidala's Naboo—has no army. His other titles include First Chairman and Viceroy of Alderaan. Bail Organa is an important figure in the overall *Star Wars* saga. He will become the foster father of Princess Leia Organa, who will serve as the Senator from Alderaan.

FOSTER FATHER KNOWS BEST
Playing Bail Organa marks Jimmy Smits's first appearance in a *Star Wars* motion picture. A well-known actor born in Brooklyn, New York, and raised in Puerto Rico, he has had memorable roles in two top-rated television series, *L.A. Law* and *NYPD Blue*.

SENIOR REPRESENTATIVE JAR JAR BINKS
Once an outcast among his fellow Gungans, Jar Jar Binks became a hero of the Battle of Naboo. Now a Senior Representative of Naboo, he has come a long way from his clumsy youth. Even Boss Nass, the leader of the Gungans, has expressed his pride in Jar Jar's evolution into a diplomat. Like Senator Amidala, he is a Loyalist. But for all the praise that has been heaped upon him, Jar Jar remains modest but sadly gullible. Made to think he is doing the best thing for the Republic, he is duped into giving Palpatine the opening he needs to assume emergency powers and invoke the Military Creation Act. Where will it all lead? The future is clouded, according to Yoda, but the dark side is certainly on the horizon.

"Deesa bad times, bombad times."
—Jar Jar Binks

SENATOR ONACONDA FARR
A Rodian from Rodia, Senator Onaconda Farr is an expert at shifting blame to others.

MAS AMEDDA
A Chagrian from Champala, Mas Amedda is Palpatine's aide and the Senate speaker.

SENATOR ASK AAK
A Gran from Malastare, Senator Ask Aak is in favor of creating a standing army for the Republic.

SENATOR TUNDRA DOWMEIA
A Quarren from Mon Calamari, this Senator is in a faction opposed to that of corrupt Quarren Senator Tikkes.

SENATOR ORN FREE TAA
A Twi'lek from Ryloth, Senator Orn Free Taa is the ringleader of a large faction of corrupt Senators. He is strongly in favor of war with the Separatists.

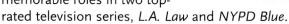

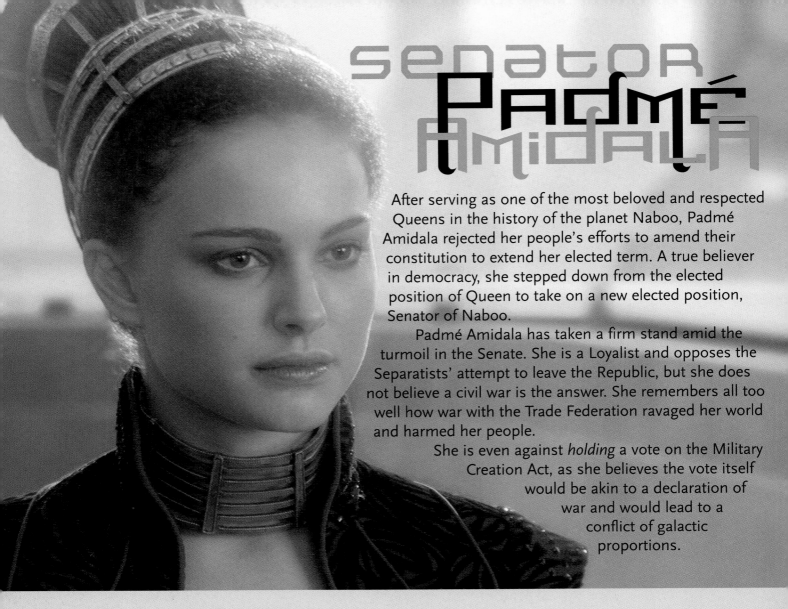

senator Padmé Amidala

After serving as one of the most beloved and respected Queens in the history of the planet Naboo, Padmé Amidala rejected her people's efforts to amend their constitution to extend her elected term. A true believer in democracy, she stepped down from the elected position of Queen to take on a new elected position, Senator of Naboo.

Padmé Amidala has taken a firm stand amid the turmoil in the Senate. She is a Loyalist and opposes the Separatists' attempt to leave the Republic, but she does not believe a civil war is the answer. She remembers all too well how war with the Trade Federation ravaged her world and harmed her people.

She is even against *holding* a vote on the Military Creation Act, as she believes the vote itself would be akin to a declaration of war and would lead to a conflict of galactic proportions.

THE NABOO SENATOR'S WARDROBE

Although Padmé Amidala is no longer Queen of Naboo, the position of Senator is regarded as highly important, as is reflected by her elaborate wardrobe.

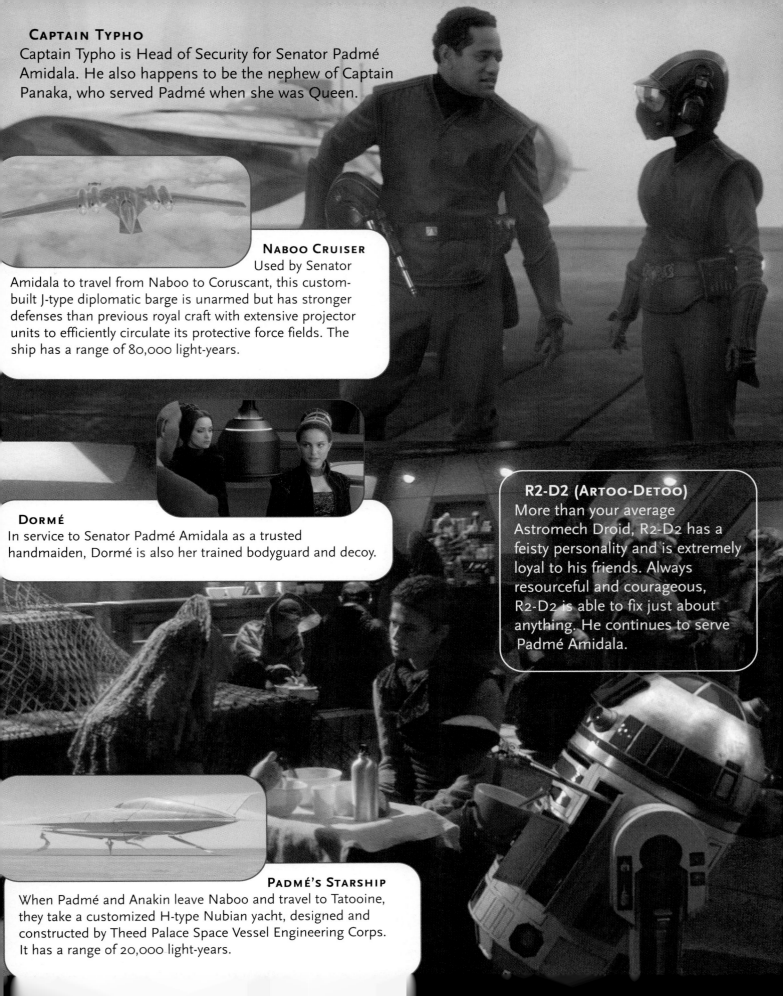

CAPTAIN TYPHO

Captain Typho is Head of Security for Senator Padmé Amidala. He also happens to be the nephew of Captain Panaka, who served Padmé when she was Queen.

NABOO CRUISER

Used by Senator Amidala to travel from Naboo to Coruscant, this custom-built J-type diplomatic barge is unarmed but has stronger defenses than previous royal craft with extensive projector units to efficiently circulate its protective force fields. The ship has a range of 80,000 light-years.

DORMÉ

In service to Senator Padmé Amidala as a trusted handmaiden, Dormé is also her trained bodyguard and decoy.

R2-D2 (ARTOO-DETOO)

More than your average Astromech Droid, R2-D2 has a feisty personality and is extremely loyal to his friends. Always resourceful and courageous, R2-D2 is able to fix just about anything. He continues to serve Padmé Amidala.

PADMÉ'S STARSHIP

When Padmé and Anakin leave Naboo and travel to Tatooine, they take a customized H-type Nubian yacht, designed and constructed by Theed Palace Space Vessel Engineering Corps. It has a range of 20,000 light-years.

CORUSCANT UNDERGROUND

From a distance, the glittering kilometer-high skyscrapers that cover the entire surface of Coruscant make it look like an urban jungle, but the story of this planet is really a tale of two worlds.

On the higher floors of these megastructures, those citizens who possess wealth, fame, or high-level government jobs live in large, luxurious apartments and breathe purified air. In the lower levels, however, life is spent toiling at menial jobs and living in cramped quarters with artificial light and anonymous neighbors of unknown species.

Go still one or two levels lower and you'll find a thriving underbelly of cutthroats, con artists, scavengers, and a general mix of galactic riffraff. When Obi-Wan and Anakin hunt an elusive assassin amid the maze of megabuildings, they are not surprised when their pursuit leads them into the Outlander, a nightclub frequented by dozens of such suspicious-looking characters. They know that on a world where a thousand species and races come together to do business, an unsavory element is an inevitability.

HAT LO

Hat Lo encourages the belief that he controls a vast criminal network on Coruscant. In fact, he is nothing more than a lackey for a powerful Hutt, who has lately grown very annoyed by reports of Hat Lo's bragging.

ELAN SLEAZEBAGGANO

Elan Sleazebaggano uses his rudimentary knowledge of alien psychology to hustle contraband. He believes his oily style, embarrassing dance moves, and occasionally successful sleights of hand (learned during his brief time with a troupe of trickster players) are what bolsters his popularity. In actuality, the underground crowd tolerates his parasitic company for one reason: the addictive death sticks he peddles for crime boss Hat Lo.

THE OUTLANDER CLUB
NIGHTCLUB PATRONS

DANNL FAYTONNI

A con man from Corellia, Dannl Faytonni attracts women even when he isn't disguised as a Lieutenant of Coruscant's Republic Guard. After a mysterious beauty whispers some very confidential information in his ear, he decides to relieve Hat Lo of everything he owns.

Dex's Diner

DEXTER JETTSTER
Once a prospector at a mining system beyond the Outer Rim, Dexter Jettster is now the owner of Dex's Diner. Possessing an uncanny memory, he is also a valued friend of Obi-Wan's, who relies on Dexter as a credible source of bizarre information.

WA-7
A Waitress Droid, WA-7 dislikes low tippers and is often seen shamelessly flirting with the dishwasher unit.

AYY VIDA
Ayy Vida has long been one of Hat Lo's consorts, but the only thing that prevents her from leaving him is her fear of the ruthless Tas Kee. When a dapper Republic Guard enters the nightclub, it's love at first sight for the Twi'lek.

ACHK MED-BEQ
Achk Med-Beq is the ambitious and inventive friend of Dannl Faytonni. He's supposed to be watching his partner's back, but he's distracted by the gaze of a mysterious woman with deathly pale skin.

TAS KEE
A Weequay from Sriluur, Tas Kee is Hat Lo's enforcer. She routinely carries several concealed weapons, all of which are designed to evade standard detectors.

Bounty Hunters

JETPACK
Jango's jetpack is a combination rocket launcher and jumper-pack. The launcher can fire either a missile or a grappling hook, and the jet jumper system is used for short flights to escape enemies or to surprise prey.

JANGO FETT

Widely regarded as the best bounty hunter in the galaxy, Jango Fett never shies away from difficult assignments. Although much of his work goes unreported, several of his more notorious exploits have become the stuff of legend among law-enforcement officers and criminals alike. After the death of his parents, he became involved with the Mandalorians, a group of soldiers-for-hire legendary for their fighting abilities. This dangerous army was eventually vanquished by the Jedi, but Jango refused to give up the trademark armor. Keeping himself in top physical and mental condition, Jango has become the ultimate lone warrior.

"I'm just a simple man, trying to make my way in the universe."—Jango Fett

WEAPONS
An array of weapons is hidden within Jango Fett's armor. They include kneepad rocket-dart launchers, arm and wrist gauntlets, and hidden blades. His blasters are Westar-34s, custom-made and perfectly balanced for his hands. They are made of an alloy that can withstand heat that would melt a standard weapon.

ARMOR
Jango Fett's Mandalorian armor is engineered to dissipate attacks from energized weapons, such as high-powered blasters and lightsabers. Beneath his chest- and thigh-blast armor, Jango wears a reinforced double-layered flight suit. Armor-mesh gloves and tough boots also provide protection.

DRAWING BOARD—THE FETT LOOK
Jango's trademark Mandalorian armor is basically a non-tarnished, non-battered version of what we originally saw his "son," Boba Fett, wear in *The Empire Strikes Back* and *Return of the Jedi.* That look was developed by conceptual artist Ralph McQuarrie and art director/visual-effects creator Joe Johnston. "I painted Boba's outfit and tried to make it look like it was made of different pieces of armor," said Johnston. "It was a symmetrical design, but I painted it in such a way that it looked like he had scavenged parts and had done some personalizing of his costume."

KAMINO SABERDART
A toxic dart used by Jango, the saberdart has tiny cuts that distinguish it as an item with origins on the planet Kamino. Strangely, there are no records regarding Kamino at the Jedi Temple.

Slave I

Built by Kuat Systems Engineering for Outer Rim police patrols, this *Firespray*-class starship was acquired by Jango Fett about the time of the Battle of Naboo. Protected with powerful shields and equipped with tracking devices, it is also packed with an array of weapons that include blaster cannons, proton torpedoes, and sonic charges that can be dropped like mines to discourage pursuers.

Drawing Board—*Slave I*

Nilo Rodis-Jamero, assistant art director and visual-effects creator for *The Empire Strikes Back,* originally designed Boba Fett's ship, *Slave I* (previously owned by Jango). "I remember seeing a radar dish and stopping to sketch it very quickly to see if I could get something out of it. When we were building the ships at ILM [Industrial Light & Magic, George Lucas's special-effects company], somebody looked at street lamps and pointed out that they looked like Boba's ship. So everyone began to think that was where I got the idea for the design."

As a Clawdite, Zam Wesell is able to shape-shift at will, a talent she puts to good use as a bounty hunter and professional assassin. Besides being able to assume the appearance of nearly any species, she is also an expert tracker and bomb-maker. It's no wonder Jango hires her to help him complete his latest assassination mission!

Kouhuns

These poisonous, centipede-like creatures called kouhuns are given to Zam by Jango Fett, who has hired her to help him do away with Senator Amidala.

Zam's Airspeeder

This *Koro*-2 all-environment exodrive airspeeder is not weighed down by weapons. Built for use on primitive and hostile worlds, this repulsorlift speeder is totally self-enclosed, with a two-week air supply. Forward mandibles operate as an external electromagnetic-propulsion system, driving the vehicle to a top speed of 800 kilometers per hour. One of the side effects of its operation is noxious gases that leave a foul smell in breathable atmospheres.

Assassin/Sentry Droid

Zam's ASN-121 Assassin Droid is equipped with spy sensors as well as a repulsorlift engine that allows it to fly. It also carries a variety of weapons and tools, including flamethrowers, a harpoon gun, a gas dispenser, and an array of drills and cutters. Its nose holds a canister dispenser in which Zam places deadly kouhuns.

MODEL SOLDIER

JANGO FETT

Although Jango Fett uses many exotic weapons and devices as a bounty hunter, his greatest asset is his own mental and physical conditioning. Possessing unusually fast reflexes and a high threshold for pain, he is absolutely fearless and able to remain calm during extreme circumstances.

Reports of Jango Fett's incredible abilities reached the attention of certain individuals who sought a "host" from whom they could clone an army of soldiers for the Republic. These soldier clones would be genetically engineered to follow any order without question, and they would age to maturity within ten years. After Jango Fett was recruited for the job by a mysterious man named Tyranus on one of the moons of Bogden, he agreed to be the clones' template—for a considerable fee, of course.

BOBA FETT

Jango Fett demanded more than just a fee for the use of his genetic pattern. He also asked for an unaltered clone of himself, a near-perfect reproduction without independency inhibitors or growth acceleration. He named this particular clone "Boba," and refers to the boy—now ten years old—as his "son." Most beings regard Jango Fett as a ruthless man, and would be surprised by his apparent devotion to Boba. More cynical beings, however, might suspect that Boba is nothing more than the ultimate embodiment of Jango Fett's supreme sense of self-preservation.

Indeed, young Boba has not only inherited all of Jango Fett's physical and psychological strengths, but he has also had the additional advantage of being raised and educated by the ultimate bounty hunter. Despite his age, Boba Fett already knows much about the arts of war, hunting, and survival.

A Bounty Hunter's Legacy

Following in Jango Fett's footsteps, Boba Fett will also come to be known as the most notorious bounty hunter in the galaxy. Here are a few of his future jobs:

Tatooine gangster Jabba the Hutt will hire Boba Fett to capture Han Solo, captain of the *Millennium Falcon,* after Han fails to deliver an expensive shipment of spice.

Sith Lord Darth Vader will commission Boba Fett to find and capture the crew of the *Millennium Falcon.* Vader is hoping his son, Luke Skywalker, will be among those snagged.

Eventually, under the burning suns of Tatooine, the "son" of Jango Fett will face off against the son of Anakin Skywalker (Episode VI: *Return of the Jedi*).

BOUNTY HUNTERS' CREED

NO HUNTER SHALL KILL

ANOTHER HUNTER

OR INTERFERE WITH

ANOTHER'S HUNT.

This creed is widely observed by the Bounty Hunters' Guild and, surprisingly, by even the most unethical of bounty hunters.

How George Lucas Created Boba Fett

When George Lucas began working on his early scripts for *Star Wars,* he was uncertain about Darth Vader's background. "I wanted to develop an essentially evil, very frightening character. He started as a kind of intergalactic bounty hunter, evolved into a grotesque knight, and, as I got deeper into the knight ethos, he became more a dark warrior than a mercenary. I split him up, and it was from the early concept of Darth Vader as a bounty hunter that Boba Fett came."

KAMINO

Hoping to identify the culprits behind the plot to kill Senator Amidala, Obi-Wan Kenobi goes to the storm-shrouded planet of Kamino.

The Kaminoans were once a land-based species, but their planet's melting ice caps forced them to build their cities on towering platforms. Their struggle to survive eventually led them to cloning, which they have used not only to maintain their species but also to perfect it. They despise mental or physical weakness, and have little interest in life beyond their star system.

However, they have occasionally agreed to create clones for beings from other worlds. On the planet Subterrel in the Outer Rim Territories, Kaminoan-produced clone miners were used for many years. Still, few outlanders are aware that Kamino even exists.

PRIME MINISTER LAMA SU
As the leader of the Kaminoans, Lama Su is very proud of the excellent cloning work done on his planet. He is practically gleeful at Obi-Wan's arrival and informs him that the Republic's clone army is nearly ready. This is news to Obi-Wan, who instantly realizes that there have been very secret dealings on Kamino.

"Clones can think creatively. You'll find that they are immensely superior to droids."
—Lama Su

AIWHAS
Native creatures of Naboo, aiwhas are flying cetaceans. Ideal transports on watery planets, they use their wide wings and powerful pectoral muscles to propel themselves under the water or through the air. Although historical records suggest that aiwhas were once imported to Kamino from Naboo, there is some speculation that Kamino's aiwha population is entirely the result of cloning technology.

TIPOCA CITY

Resting on great stilts, the huge city of Tipoca rises above the ever-present waves that cover the surface of this watery world. Constantly lashed by heavy rains and hard-driving winds, Tipoca City's architecture does not embrace the elements but rather openly defies them.

TAUN WE

A Kaminoan aide to the Prime Minister of Kamino, Taun We warmly welcomes Obi-Wan to her planet and tells him that his arrival has been long expected. Because Obi-Wan has only recently learned of Kamino's existence, he is both puzzled and intrigued by this reception.

According to Prime Minister Lama Su, Kamino was visited ten years ago by a Jedi Master named Sifo-Dyas, who placed an order for a clone army to serve the Republic.

Obi-Wan recognizes the name Sifo-Dyas. He was indeed a Jedi Master, but he was killed about ten years earlier! Obi-Wan is perplexed by this mystery, but the fact remains that the order was placed, and the Kaminoans have honored it. The result is that 200,000 clones are ready and another million are well on the way.

Lama Su and Taun We present the clone army to Obi-Wan.

"Magnificent, aren't they?"—Lama Su

WHAT IS A CLONE?

Kaminoans have become experts in cloning technology. What is a clone? Unlike most living creatures, which are the products of male and female parents, a clone is a reproduction of a single being, "grown" from a single bodily cell of that being. Genetically identical to his or her parent, the young clone grows to greatly resemble him or her, although it is not born with the same memories.

Identical in physical appearance, mental capacity, and stamina, the clone troopers are virtually indistinguishable from one another. All are clad in white armor that protects them from projectile and impact weapons, glancing blaster bolts, and harsh environments.

CLONE TROOPER
NO.214736184505796

CLONE CENTER VISIT

Obi-Wan tours the facilities where the clone troopers are created. By using growth-acceleration technology, the Kaminoans are able to grow clone troopers (from a single cell to adulthood) in half the time it would take for an ordinary clone to mature. A fully formed clone trooper can be produced in ten years.

CLONE CENTER CLASSROOM

Clone troopers are schooled from an early age. Because of the independency inhibitors introduced into their genetic code, they are completely obedient and will never disagree or argue with a teacher.

CLONE TROOPERS

TIPOCA CITY PARADE GROUNDS
Though genetically engineered to be perfect soldiers, the clones still require extensive training before they are prepared to fight for the Republic. Marching and drilling under the brutal rain and winds of Kamino, they quickly evolve into battle-hardened warriors.

CLONE CENTER COMMISSARY
Clones digest food and breathe in the same manner as their genetic host. Unlike the host, these clone troopers are totally obedient and will take any order from their superiors without question or argument.

"Do you like your army? . . . They'll do their job well. I'll guarantee that."—Jango Fett

JANGO'S APARTMENT
Taun We takes Obi-Wan to the apartment of Jango Fett, the "host" for the clone army.

CLONE TROOPER

THEED PALACE

Built at the edge of a great plateau, the city of Theed is the capital city of Naboo and the crown jewel of its civilization. Once the residence of Queen Amidala, Theed Palace is now inhabited by Queen Jamillia.

CORUSCANT FREIGHTER

Jedi Padawan Anakin Skywalker embarks on his first solo mission when the Jedi Council orders him to escort Padmé Amidala back to her homeworld. Assassins are threatening her life on Coruscant, and Anakin is to provide protection. To maintain secrecy, they disguise themselves as outland peasants and travel on a Coruscant starfreighter loaded with emigrants. R2-D2, who is always reliable in dangerous situations, accompanies them to Naboo.

Queen Jamillia

Jamillia, elected leader of Naboo, began her reign after Padmé Amidala had completed her two terms, the maximum number of terms allowed. Although she is relieved to see Padmé alive and well, Jamillia is concerned by reports of the many systems that have joined Count Dooku and the Separatists.

"We must keep our faith in the Republic. The day we stop believing democracy can work is the day we lose it."
—Queen Jamillia

Disguised as peasants, Anakin and Amidala pay a visit to Theed Palace.

Sio Bibble

Governor of Theed, Bibble was a member of the Royal Advisory Council when Padmé Amidala was Queen. He continues to serve as a trusted adviser to Queen Jamillia.

Where on Earth Is Naboo?

While most live-action scenes for Episode II were filmed at Fox Studios Australia in Sydney and Ealing Studios in England, some of the Naboo scenes were filmed in Caserta, Italy, a location that was previously used in *The Phantom Menace*. Other scenes were filmed at the Plaza de España in Seville, Spain, where the cast and crew were greeted by more than 3,000 fans.

Naboo Lake Retreat

Surrounded by a shimmering lake, an island lodge becomes a temporary sanctuary for Padmé and Anakin. They had hoped the remote location would simply provide protection, but the beautiful area also inspires powerful emotions. As Padmé is completely dedicated to helping Naboo and Anakin is studying to become a Jedi Knight, neither is entirely prepared to deal with their increasingly strong feelings of mutual attraction.

WHERE ON EARTH IS THE NABOO LAKE RETREAT?
The Naboo lake retreat scenes were filmed at some of the villas and gardens around Lake Como, Italy. According to George Lucas, "There are many places here in Italy that are unlike any place else in the world."

"From the moment I met you, all those years ago, a day hasn't gone by when I haven't thought of you."
—Anakin Skywalker

"If you follow your thoughts through to conclusion, they will take us to a place we cannot go . . . regardless of the way we feel about each other."
—Padmé Amidala

MOUNTAIN MEADOW

Embracing the traditional recreational activities that are offered at the retreat, Padmé and Anakin spend an afternoon exploring the nearby meadows.

LODGE DINING ROOM

A lovely view of the lake provides a romantic atmosphere as Padmé and Anakin share a meal.

RETURN TO TATOOINE

Located in the Outer Rim Territories, far from Republic space, Tatooine is the homeworld of the small, junk-collecting Jawas, as well as their mortal enemies, the Tusken Raiders. Tatooine's harsh environment discourages colonization, but by using vaporators to retrieve water vapor from the planet's arid atmosphere, some outlanders have managed to survive.

Anakin Skywalker spent the first eight years of his childhood as a slave on Tatooine. After ten years away, he now returns for the first time since he left to become a Jedi. Haunted by dreams of his mother, Shmi Skywalker, in danger, he is determined to find her and make certain she is safe.

WATTO
In the city of Mos Espa, Anakin goes to see his former owner, Watto the Toydarian. Watto still operates his repair shop, but no longer owns any slaves, having sold Shmi years ago to a moisture farmer named Lars. According to Watto, the farmer fell in love with Shmi and bought her in order to free her.

DOWN ON THE FARM
The young Owen Lars (Joel Edgerton) and his girlfriend, Beru Whitesun (Bonnie Piesse), are happy in their lives working the Lars moisture farm near Mos Eisley on Tatooine. Neither has any desire to go anywhere else in the galaxy.

OWEN LARS' SWOOP BIKE
Sensing his mother is still alive, Anakin borrows Owen's repulsorlift speeder to travel over the desert and track her abductors. A helpful Jawa directs Anakin to the Tusken Raider camp.

Lars Homestead

At the Lars moisture farm, Anakin and Padmé are reunited with Anakin's droid, C-3PO. They are also introduced to Cliegg Lars, the farmer who married Shmi; Owen Lars, son of Cliegg; and Beru Whitesun, Owen's girlfriend. Cliegg reveals that Shmi has been captured by Tusken Raiders, and that he, along with many others, was injured in an attempt to rescue her.

Although Anakin and the Larses never learn why Shmi was taken by the Tusken Raiders, many Tatooine colonists come up with theories of their own. It is widely known that Tusken Raiders believe their civilization to be threatened by the increased presence of foreign outlanders, specifically human colonists.

C-3PO Restored

Shmi Skywalker gave C-3PO his coverings while she was still a slave, completing the work that her son had started. The result is less than brilliant, but the Protocol Droid is very relieved to be completed.

Years Later

Many hard years later, an older "Uncle" Owen (Phil Brown) and "Aunt" Beru (Shelagh Fraser) have become the guardian of Anakin's son, Luke Skywalker—who, unlike them, has a burning desire to see life beyond the Outer Rim world of Tatooine.

Tusken Raiders

Tatooine's desert wastelands, the Dune Sea and the Jundland Wastes, are the domain of nomadic warriors. Although their true names are known only to themselves, they are commonly referred to by Tatooine's colonists as the Sand People or Tusken Raiders. The latter name is centuries old, derived from the notoriously violent assault on one of Tatooine's first human settlements, Fort Tusken.

Some anthropologists have suggested that Fort Tusken had been built on land that was sacred to the nomads, but most contemporary colonists maintain that the Sand People have always attacked without provocation. Over the years, tensions have only increased between colonists and the so-called "Tuskens."

To keep moisture trapped near their bodies, Tusken Raiders cover themselves from head to toe in strips of cloth and tattered, gauzy robes. Their eyes are concealed by tubelike goggles with protective lenses, and breath filters prevent them from inhaling sand particles.

TUSKEN RAIDER CAMP
Tatooine's human colonists would shudder at the nightmarish thought of arriving upon an entire camp of Sand People. It is here that Anakin's search for his mother ends.

GADERFFI STICK
Assembled from scavenged metal parts, the gaderffi stick—also called a gaffi—is the traditional weapon of Tusken Raiders. To ensure that it inflicts fatal wounds, its sharp point is dipped in poison.

"Those Tuskens walk like men, but they're vicious, mindless monsters."
—Cliegg Lars

MASSIFF
Large lizards with sharp fangs, massiffs have been sighted prowling the dunes of Tatooine.

Fun in the sun: Actors Bonnie Piesse (far left), Joel Edgerton, and Jack Thompson relax between takes.

WHERE ON EARTH IS TATOOINE?
The Tatooine scenes were filmed in Tunisia, a republic in northern Africa. This location has been used as Tatooine in two previous *Star Wars* films, *A New Hope* and *The Phantom Menace*. How did R2-D2 react to his return to Tunisia? According to the droid's operator, Don Bies, "R2-D2 is having déjà vu."

Geonosis

Obi-Wan's hunt for a deadly bounty hunter brings him to Geonosis, which is ringed by an asteroid field. As Obi-Wan approaches the world, he sees a large fleet of Trade Federation ships. After he lands his Delta-7 starfighter, he finds the planetary surface is characterized by towering spires of red rock, many of which have been modified for habitation by the natives.

The Geonosians
Insect-like bipeds, the winged Geonosians are divided into two classes—aristocrat and warrior. A third class is represented by wingless worker drones, who labor in the foundries but do not carry weapons or participate in battle. Although Geonosians build weapons and droids in the foundries and test them, they do not have their own organized army.

Droid Factory

In a huge underground facility, automated machines construct Battle Droids while Geonosian drones work at the assembly lines.

Like the relatively nearby planet Tatooine, Geonosis is far from Coruscant and the control of the Republic. This makes it a good location to build a droid army and an ideal base for Count Dooku, the leader of the Separatist movement.

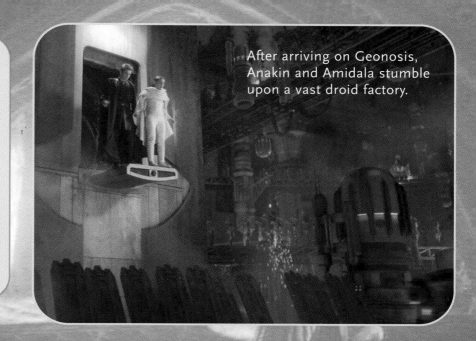

After arriving on Geonosis, Anakin and Amidala stumble upon a vast droid factory.

Swarmed by Geonosians, Anakin must fight his way out.

A Geonosian aims a sonic blaster.

EXECUTION ARENA

On Geonosis, justice is harsh and all disputes are settled in the arena! After Obi-Wan Kenobi falls into the clutches of the Separatists, Anakin, Padmé, R2-D2, and C-3PO race to Geonosis. Unfortunately, they too are captured, and all are charged with espionage against the sovereign system of Geonosis. Sentenced to death, they are placed in a large arena with three horrifying beasts.

REEK
The massive bull-like reek uses its size to intimidate Anakin and then it charges, using its horns for a lethal attack.

NEXU
Setting its eyes on Padmé, the nexu roars and displays wicked, dripping fangs.

ACKLAY
A surprisingly agile creature, the acklay angles its powerful claws to strike out at Obi-Wan.

THE CLONE WARS

The arrival on Geonosis of massive Republic assault ships filled with Republic gunships and thousands of clone troopers is the event that begins the legendary "Clone Wars." It marks the first time since its inception that the Republic has deployed an army. The ships themselves were built by Rothana Heavy Engineering, a subsidiary of Kuat. The Kuat industrialists support the Republic and not the Separatists, primarily because of their hatred of the treacherous Neimoidians, who assassinated leading Kuati executives ten years before.

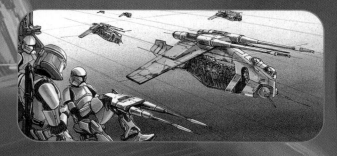

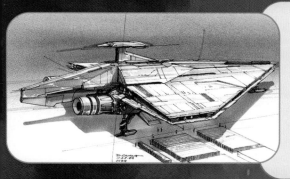

REPUBLIC ASSAULT SHIP

Assault ships are enlisted by the Republic to transport the Jedi, the clone troopers, and their equipment through deep space. These *Acclamator*-class transgalactic military transport ships are equipped with 12 quad turbolaser turrets, 24 point-defense laser cannons, and 4 missile/torpedo launch tubes. These massive vessels can carry 16,000 troopers and numerous armored vehicles over a range of 250,000 light-years.

REPUBLIC GUNSHIP

The Galactic Republic's LAAT/i (low-altitude assault transport/infantry) aerial gunships can cross rough terrain and carry armored vehicles and troops. They are lighter and faster than most mobile artillery and are equipped with 2 missile launchers, 4 rotating blaster-cannons, and 3 laser cannons. In emergencies, the entire cockpit section ejects as an escape capsule.

DRAWING BOARD

The design of the Republic gunship began with guidance from filmmaker George Lucas. "George wanted these [Republic gunships] to be helicopter-like flying vehicles," said concept designer Doug Chiang. The battered-design style for the gunships, as well as the other Republic vehicles, reflects the "used universe" feel of the original saga, which subtly foreshadows events to come.

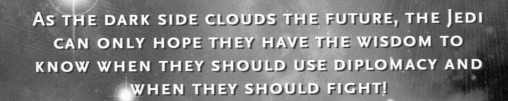

As the dark side clouds the future, the Jedi can only hope they have the wisdom to know when they should use diplomacy and when they should fight!

The Clone Wars have begun. . . .

About the Author

Ryder Windham's numerous *Star Wars* books include *The Phantom Menace Scrapbook* (Random House) and the comic book serial *Qui-Gon & Obi-Wan: Last Stand on Ord Mantell* (Dark Horse Comics). He has also written *What You Don't Know About Animals* (Scholastic) and other educational books.

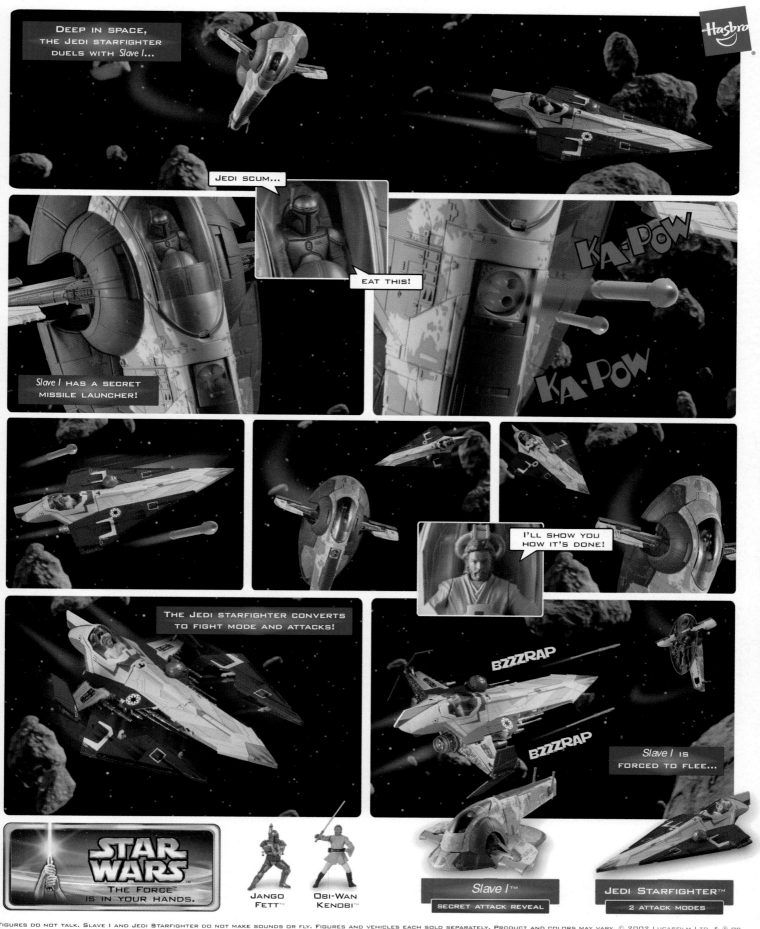

STAR WARS®
ATTACK OF THE CLONES™

Win Hasbro *Star Wars: Attack of the Clones* Holiday Toys . . . in July!

Including action figures, playsets, electronic figures, and vehicles all before they're in stores!†

Exclusive Offer!

The saga continues with the new *Star Wars* movie, *Attack of the Clones*. Random House is giving you the chance to win all-new *Attack of the Clones* Hasbro toys before they officially hit stores.† Draw a picture of a beloved *Star Wars: Attack of the Clones* character for your chance to win. Some restrictions apply. See official contest rules and eligibility requirements to find out which character to draw and complete details.

Log on to starwars.com for the latest *exclusive* information on *Star Wars: Attack of the Clones*.

www.starwars.com
www.starwarskids.com
www.randomhouse.com/kids/starwars
www.starwars.hasbro.com

Win *Star Wars* Action Figures and More!
Official Rules & Regulations

I. HOW TO ENTER

NO PURCHASE NECESSARY. Enter by printing your full name, address, phone number, and date of birth on a piece of paper, and send it to us along with the drawing required for your age group as follows: If you will be at least 5 years old but not yet 9 years old as of June 30, 2002, draw a picture of R2D2. If you will be at least 9 but not yet 12 as of June 30, 2002, draw a picture of Yoda. If you will be at least 12 but not yet 16 as of June 30, 2002, draw a picture of Jango Fett. If you will be at least 16 but not yet 19, draw a picture of Anakin from *Star Wars: Attack of the Clones*. Mail your picture to *Star Wars: Attack of the Clones* Contest, Random House Children's Books Marketing Department, 1540 Broadway, 19th Floor, New York, NY 10036. Entries must be mailed separately and received by Random House no later than June 30, 2002. LIMIT ONE ENTRY PER PERSON. Partially completed or illegible entries will not be accepted. Sponsors are not responsible for lost, late, mutilated, illegible, stolen, postage-due, incomplete, or misdirected entries. All entries become the property of Random House and will not be returned, so please keep a copy for your records.

II. ELIGIBILITY

Contest is open to all legal residents of the United States, excluding the state of Arizona and Puerto Rico, and to legal residents of Canada, excluding the Province of Quebec, who are between the ages of 5 and 18 as of June 30, 2002. All federal, state, and local laws and regulations apply. Void wherever prohibited or restricted by law. Employees of Random House Inc., Lucasfilm Ltd., Hasbro Inc., and their respective parent companies, assigns, subsidiaries or affiliates; advertising, promotion, and fulfillment agencies; and their immediate families and persons living in their household are not eligible to enter this contest.

III. PRIZES

One first place winner in age group 5–8 will win Republic Gunship, 12" Electronic Action Figure Obi-Wan, 12" Electronic Action Figure Jango, Arena Playset, and Deluxe Yoda Figure (approximate retail value $150.00 U.S.) and the winning entry will be eligible to be published in *Star Wars: Attack of the Clones Coloring Book* (on sale fall 2002). One second place winner in age group 5–8 will win Arena Playset and Deluxe Droid Factory with C-3PO (approximate retail value $50.00 U.S.). One third place winner in age group 5–8 will win Deluxe Droid Factory with C-3PO and Basic Action Figure Anakin Skywalker

(approximate retail value $16.00 U.S.). One first place winner in age group 9–11 will win Republic Gunship, 12" Electronic Action Figure Obi-Wan, 12" Electronic Action Figure Jango, Arena Playset, and Deluxe Yoda Figure (approximate retail value $150.00 U.S.) and the winning entry will be eligible to be published in *Star Wars: Attack of the Clones Coloring Book* (on sale fall 2002). One second place winner in age group 9–11 will win Arena Playset and Deluxe Droid Factory with C-3PO (approximate retail value $50.00 U.S.). One third place winner in age group 9–11 will win Deluxe Droid Factory with C-3PO and Basic Action Figure Anakin Skywalker (approximate retail value $16.00 U.S.). One first place winner in age group 12–15 will win Republic Gunship, 12" Electronic Action Figure Obi-Wan, 12" Electronic Action Figure Jango, Arena Playset, and Star Wars Unleashed Mace Windu (approximate retail value $155.00 U.S.) and the winning entry will be eligible to be published in *Star Wars: Attack of the Clones Coloring Book* (on sale fall 2002). One second place winner in age group 12–15 will win Arena Playset and Star Wars Unleashed Mace Windu (approximate retail value $55.00 U.S.). One third place winner in age group 12–15 will win Star Wars Unleashed Mace Windu and Basic Action Figure Anakin Skywalker (approximate retail value $21.00 U.S.). One first place winner in age group 16–18 will win Republic Gunship, 12" Electronic Action Figure Obi-Wan, 12" Electronic Action Figure Jango, Arena Playset, and Star Wars Unleashed Mace Windu (approximate retail value $155.00 U.S.) and the winning entry will be eligible to be published in *Star Wars: Attack of the Clones Coloring Book* (on sale fall 2002). One second place winner in age group 16–18 will win Arena Playset and Star Wars Unleashed Mace Windu (approximate retail value $55.00 U.S.). One third place winner in age group 16–18 will win Star Wars Unleashed Mace Windu and Basic Action Figure Anakin Skywalker (approximate retail value $21.00 U.S.). If for any reason a prize is not available or cannot be fulfilled, Random House Inc. reserves the right to substitute a prize of equal or greater value, including—but not limited to—cash equivalent, which is at the complete discretion of Random House Inc. Taxes, if any, are the winner's sole responsibility. Prizes are not transferable and cannot be assigned. No prize or cash substitutes allowed, except at the discretion of the sponsor as set forth above. Random House Inc., Lucasfilm Ltd., and Hasbro Inc. are not responsible if the official on-sale date of the Hasbro toys is moved up to a date earlier than the distribution of the prizes. Names of actual prizes are subject to change. The on-sale date of the *Star Wars: Attack of the Clones Coloring Book* is subject to change.

IV. WINNERS

One first place, one second place, and one third place winner will be selected in each age category on or about July 10, 2002, from all eligible entries received within the entry deadline. Winners will be selected by Random House Children's Books Marketing Department staff on the basis of creativity and originality. By participating, entrants agree to be bound by the official rules and the decision of the judges, which shall be final and binding in all respects. All prizes will be awarded in the name of the winner's parent or legal guardian if winner is under age 18. Each winner and/or winner's parent or legal guardian will be notified by mail and will be required to sign and return affidavit(s) of eligibility and release of liability within 14 days of notification. A noncompliance within that time period or the return of any notification as undeliverable will result in disqualification and the selection of an alternate winner. In the event of any other noncompliance with rules and conditions, prize may be awarded to an alternate winner. Other entry names will NOT be used for subsequent mail solicitation.

V. RESERVATIONS

By participating, winner (and winner's parent/legal guardian) agrees that Random House Inc., Lucasfilm Ltd., Hasbro Inc., and their respective parent companies, assigns, subsidiaries or affiliates, and advertising, promotion, and fulfillment agencies will have no liability whatsoever, and will be held harmless by winner (and winner's parent/legal guardian) for any liability for any injuries, losses, or damages of any kind to person, including death, and property resulting in whole or in part, directly or indirectly, from the acceptance, possession, misuse, or use of the prize, or participation in this contest. By entering the contest each winner, and/or winner's parent or legal guardian as applicable, consents to the use of the winner's name, likeness, and biographical data for publicity and promotional purposes on behalf of Random House Inc. with no additional compensation or further permission (except where prohibited by law). Other entry names will NOT be used for subsequent mail solicitation. For the name of the winners in each age category, available after August 1, 2002, please send a stamped, self-addressed envelope to: *Star Wars: Attack of the Clones* Contest Winner, Random House Children's Books Marketing Department, 1540 Broadway, 19th Floor, New York, NY 10036. Washington and Vermont residents may omit return postage.